From One Encounter to the Next

to the Next

A Collection of Prose and Poetry

Susan M. Cane

abbott press®

A DIVISION OF WRITER'S DIGEST

Abbott Press books may be ordered through booksellers or by contacting:

Abbott Press
1663 Liberty Drive
Bloomington, IN 47403
www.abbottpress.com
Phone: 1-866-697-5310

ISBN: 978-1-4582-1467-6 (sc)
ISBN: 978-1-4582-1468-3 (e)

Library of Congress Control Number: 2014903743

Printed in the United States of America.

Abbott Press rev. date: 3/31/2014

Biography

I am proud to be publishing "One Encounter To the Next?" I have worked on it over the years, and I believe that now is the time to open it up to readers. I live in the beautiful state of Pennsylvania. I enjoy the old houses, the culture and the city of Philadelphia. I also study for a Master's In Business, and I have a Bachelor Degree in Psychology.

I like to spend my time pursuing artistic hobbies like oil painting, sketching, sculpting, and of course, writing.

The book was written for those who have suffered Mental Illness, but I also want to touch the soul of anyone else. Mental Health is a devastating experience, as my book will show you through fiction and poetry.

It contains stories of people with mental illness, and the experiences they go through. The poetry relates to my own experiences, and the insights I received through those experiences

Dedication

The book is a dedication to all that suffer from mental illness, and to all who want to learn.

Chapter One

I have Potential

Excerpt From Sigmund's Diary

June 30th, 1751

Today I was freed from isolation for only a few hours. I sat and watched the birds, and as I observed they seemed to be guiding my thoughts. The sun was out and this felt very happy, as I always feel melancholy and damned when it rains. But still I have learned nothing. My jacket feels like it is fitting well this morning, but right now I feel not well. Today my shoes feel smaller. But I am no lesser a man! The Doctor damned to me again, saying with a smile that he had made his decision. And the other patients, tired and frightened, watched as I left the building and went outside. To think, that I would find fault in my own decisions! What decisions has he that I should morn? But still I watch the birds and know nothing. And still, at he present, I am no lesser a man.

July 9th, 1751

Today I was taught to dress myself and take care of my personal habits. As I stood naked I could feel the eyes of the male nurses staring at my genitals. Next, while clothed only with a small covering, I could feel the humiliation. But still I could stand with a sense of dignity. One I know all to well, but could never come to realize what it was or where it came from. In uniform, I could still see the eyes glaring at me with a sense of stigma. Then I felt crazy. I felt we were all crazy. Just standing here to be crazy as they watched and proclaimed our being. My genitals were hardening as I have never felt much more than this. Then the feeling of tiny birds flashed in my eyes as I came to a happier nature. Then, at closure, I left the room to reassure and compose myself. Theirs has a dirty meaning that I must contend with everyday. This I have learned to do very well, with everyday of my life.

July 13th, 1751

Today I watched a mental embalming. The man had a jaw that was corrected to the left. I wait in a chair near the operating table, as if I were to make my own decisions. There was cutting and much blood, which squirted from the man's head. I felt to vomit, but I could only watch. The surgeon's hands would not shake a bit as I watched in comfort. My gown was fresh and new, and I waited and watched his posture very closely. But still, I knew nothing, even though there was this interest. As the surgeon was finished, the man's jaw was corrected to the right and his eyes were bulging. But he was only dismissed as the surgeon did his own writings. I was to be next, and the fear was exhilarating for it was my first. My neck tightened as I panicked and was slowly guided to the table that appeared to be a God. Everything was silent, my mind, my brain, my arms and my whole body. It was a feeling of ecstasy that I had never felt in my entire life. I only prayed that my face would not look obscure when it was over.

July 17th, 1751

Today I used my teachings of how to keep myself. The room I bathed in was extremely dirty, and I thought to myself of how I could become clean. But still I used the soap at approximately the same measurements as I was told. And though I used this much, I found the sink to be to dirty, and so was my body. My hair has no unique way, but at least it used some soap. I thought that I should hurry, for there was a long line of others waiting to use the room. So, as I left the room, I watched the faces as they saw me in complete wonder. But they did not wonder of themselves, but of my cleanliness. I smiled and nodded to show them my contentedness. I was to continue my day as usual, hoping not to be treated. To us all, treatments were a horror. But somehow, still, I had my own decisions. My God, their eyes look so tormented! They looked Hebrews waiting to be saved. Their eyes looked like that of a ghost.

July 25th, 1751

I was taken immediately this morning to see the Physist. I had only finished my cleaning, as it was the day to do so. But still I feel contaminated, and as I saw the Phyist, I felt to tell him. But his expressionless face told me not to. Again, I had no decisions. So I sat contaminated, but I could not even wonder how or why. What was it that he could be so godly? Why was it that I was so unprivileged, and his motions were so privileged? Why is it that with each question, which was asked, I had no concept of how to answer? When conference was over I was relieved. I hated to be there, in the room. And at each time when he was finished, I felt a little closer to wanting to be dead. But I am not to think that way because God says that it is a sin. So I will put my thoughts to something else. Perhaps I will take a game, or if I am fortunate, a walk.

July 30th, 1751

Today a plain closed person I have never seen visited the hospital. He seemed very tall and I could not keep myself from being in complete wonder. He was an alien. Never have I felt such complete wonder. I could not stop admiring just his smallest actions. Never have I seen such composure in one's face. I could only think of what his life was and where he came from. Was he a Prince or a Vagabond? Was I to discover the normal? Was I to learn abnormal? I left the room. I didn't want to learn the latter. The others may if they wish to. But I couldn't. I would then, surely, become lesser. They will make their decision and I will make mine. But there is such an aching in my mind to hide from them. I will go out and learn. No. No I cannot. I will stay here where they cannot forbid me. Forbid me by my knowing what I really am.

August 4th, 1751

Today I was exhausted. I could barely hold up my head. The plain clothed man had gone away. And I was left in complete wonder. Who am I? What am I? Over and over I asked these questions to myself. And although I couldn't stop wondering, my mind strained and asked me to release this horrible feeling. I felt dread. My habits where constantly nagging me. I couldn't stop neglecting the others. But still I was not out of place. His decisions, what were his decisions? What decisions did he make? And of course there was the main question. How did I seem to him? He did not know of me. But how did he see the others? Was I seeing now what he saw? Please, I begged myself, stop this way of thinking. There, one caught my eye. I will be even more in prison. What relief! He only looked away. But was that his decision or did he really know nothing at all?

August 8th, 1751

Days have passed and still I feel like a monster. It has been quite a long time and still the man was in my mind. I remember his face. I cannot forget it. And I cannot stop comparing it with my own. Mine was so stern. And in his you could see his-self. The stern in mine was not majestic. No, as I study these pictures, the sternness was not my own. It was his, the Doctors! He is in his, but mine is not. Mine had been tampered with for years. His is free flowing and adjusted, just as his life must be. My life is in a prison cell. God, I could only dream of what his might be. Gardens and walls, and people, and women I dreamed by. I myself could only dream of the women! And the clothes I imagined. What a heavy black jacket and shoes that shined! And all that I have to bare is this coat full of holes, and shoes that only were used to cover my feet. Now I was jealous. Close was the lessened of myself. If only I could stop my thoughts!

August 14th, 1751

After enormous contemplation, that Devil of a man has left my mind! You would think that there was much relief, but there was hardly any. Now that I knew more of myself I could only think of my death. With no memory of the man's face and clothes, still what were left were all the ideas I have created. I wanted death to myself so surely that mostly every minute it was what I planned. Although I was under much security, I knew that I could find ways of doing it. Why? Why did suicide never cross my mind? Maybe it was that I did not make my own decisions. But now that I saw that man, the normal man, now I have the intelligence of making up my own mind. That intelligence was suicide. I went back to my room to plan. Here I could concentrate at the night table with no distractions. But why were there no distractions here?

August 21st, 1751

Reality is eating at my brain! Just the way that he sucked at his toffee was edged into my mind once again. He sees me Looney. He laughs at my face as he enjoys the ingredients. And though this was only one day for him, it was my whole lifetime. My dreaded, unprivileged life was at the mercy of his mere expression. That is what I am. I am a crazy locked away for no reasons. But still there was no law that said I could not be. This and my reality were my thoughts for each day, every day. My mind ached to the point that I must bow to the ceilings, maybe perhaps to find an answer from any God who had one. And after not finding any answers, it was my question of the presence of any God who could damn me for taking my own life. Even though the Devil stood and watched me, I planned. Even though he craved at my fortunes, I only ignored and continued to pry against their walls, walls that stood so high that my eyes could never reach their obelisk intelligence. But still I planned with the only source I could find, my grievousness. The lustfulness of my lowliness was one subject that left not meaning, but will. It was a strong will, weakened at times, but strong enough for the act. In my misery I realized. What could I lose?

September 3rd, 1751

Today I was hardly up and around. And my depressions were unthinkable. Not only the fears of my existence, but the depressions. It was someone or something telling me to go ahead with my plans. I am lying on my deathbed now. But there was not a soul in the miserable world that cared. I felt to give in and cry, but still my stoutness keeps me from being lesser. If only I could use this feeling and live it in the real world, in freedom. But of course, I can only wonder what the real world is. I eat, sleep, bath on occasion and I am treated. Then I become ill and vomit. All of these things become a long cycle. They are cycles of depression, and mania, and while I live this way, others live at least their fortunes. God, is this not a fair reason to want to die and leave this world you have created? I do not doubt you. Your Earth is sinful. This you have proven. But why can't I leave and go to the heavens all in the same? A new thought had approached me. Not only am I a sinner, but I am also trapped! Here!

September 14th, 1751

What an honor I had! I slept in comfort last night. My thinking has turned to the Devil. I gave up on God. He didn't answer. But the Devil, he did. He has been answering me the whole time. And even intelligence has proven that in my mind was the work of the Devil. It has been his voices that I hear in my head! But while I was thinking and remembering this morning, I heard an awful noise. It was the sound of a horn. It was loud and offending. It sounded over and over. Then I was dragged from my bed and into the hall. Everywhere was people in shock. We were to be collected at the sound of the horn! One women burst into tears. Another began to yell and scream. And aloud I said," Stop it! Stop it now!" I was knocked unconscious and I awoke here! In the Devil's whelm I am living! But not for long will I! I will not be treated as an animal, or a fool. The Devil will not let me.

September 20th, 1751

What more can drag me to insanity? A priest came today to read to us a prayer. Once I have finally met my fate, God comes to stop me. Is it a message or is it meant to worsen my feelings of my intention? God, who creates the genius, came to me today and made me confused. It was the kind I knew all to well. It is why they call me Looney. Then God stands before me to make it true. And this was the Hebrew God. Is this the God of goodness and moral freedom? Where was mine? I thought a plan. I will give up to the Devil, Gods word read or not. I will ignore that which has ignored me all this time. Then the scars! Don't torment me with scars, dear God of love. Again, there was no answer. Silence, confusion, torment, search for decision all returning once again. There was a tear, and of course then confusion, which stopped it. Who was stopping it? Let it go! The Doctor, it was he! The Doctor thinks he is God. And who is to doubt? As long as I am alive, he is. But which God is he? The Devil is in my disease so he must be the divine. Or is he the Devil tormenting me? I stare at the eyes of the priest with the Devil. But his, they look so kind. A tear comes. But he is from the outside, and he has reason. I will clothe the Devil!

September 25th, 1751

Depressions save me! I want back my depressions! There are phantoms coming again and no one knows what to do! There is the doctor in my eyesight. He only laughs and does not save my life. He jeers because he has entered my eyes again. The phantom had gone and we had smiled. We had agreed that I could go on. And now the phantoms are returning. I miss my depressions by the lamplight. And I miss calmly sipping my liquids and thinking as a complete human being. Now I know that God is not on my side. But in this world full of the filthiest sinners, why am I possessed? I feel I want to explode now, or even let a cry. I want to reach out and grasp the hand of my Lord. But he is nowhere to be found. I am the phantom doctor's prisoner and I want to die. Does no one hear me? There is a knock on my door and it is he! It is the phantom he coming to jeer. In my eyes I beg of him. But then the devil left me no choice. I ran at him in a rage and forced him to the floor with my fist. He looked at me in shock and gave his powerful command that was always my most sacred fate. And then I could not move for hours. And the phantoms, they laughed at me and drew me even closer to insanity. Now nothing will obligate my plans. There is no God, I know. So there is reason to worry.

October 9th, 1751

Now I can only beg of the grave. Today my arms are leaving my sides and I must be strapped to this chair. And the most humiliating aspect is the drool that constantly drips from my chin. And the devil smiles and I don't. And now what am I to do with no God. If the doctor comes he will bring me much relief. To know that this is not he would at least bring my arm down a quarter of an inch. Then comes the jolting. The pain fragments make my arms branch out like a tree begging for water. This made me beg for the times when I am selecting attention. I would give up even my decisions to have some way to only bare this torture. And this time I cannot be relieved by the begging of my God, for he is not here, or anywhere. My legs are shrinking and are moved off to the side. And I kept hoping that the plain closed man would not come back. Did not anyone feel strange? And no one gives me medicine. I would love to clench their throats, grieve out their medicines, and take their medicines away. I became a crazy man sitting like that of a man in denial. But this was only for a second because it was too small. As my leg shakes slightly, the doctor moves into the room. Then my whole body trembled and was completely out of control. I felt as if I was a child. He ignores me, but at least he is here and in not the phantoms.

October 14th, 1751

Now I know the meaning of relief! Now I know my God! The restraint was taken away. And at that moment I found God. My whole body lapsed into freedom that reached my brain. To be in agony such a long time constantly and then be freed was the most I have ever felt. Even my genitals were relieved. Now I know how Jesus must have felt when he passed on to heaven. And to leave the chair and walk was ecstasy, although movement was dragging my feet. Even the lustfulness as I moved by the others was better than that restricting chair. I would only pray that it never happens again. And as I fell to my knees I realized, I am now weak. I was taken to my room. I lye awake for moments trying to recapture that moment of the past. I couldn't sleep. I told the nurses I could not sleep. They offered me medicine and I took it. Then I slept for days. Then when I awoke I found a card on my table. It portrayed a picture of Jesus. Then I let a cry, and then returned to my prayer. The Devil is the God of pain. Now I knew that. I returned to my God, Yahweh. The God of immortal love is he. The message? I am.

October 18th, 1751

Today, in my robe, I made time for dinner. I ate with a smile and I have not even yet begun to pray. And all seems better except for this pain I get in the back of my head. It doesn't seem to portray any of the Phantoms at the present. So at the time I finish I will return to pray. There, I have picked up the last part of my food. Now I will walk through the halls to my room. The halls are rectangular and straight, as is much of the hospital's structure. And at times were people who would chose spots to dwell in. But I spend more time in my room where I can pray. Then, in the door at the end came the plain closed man from God knows where? He came perhaps from some place on a mountain, to come in and find me here. He came in white uniform that doesn't reach his knees. And his legs strived in his black shoes and silver garnish that I have never seen. Was it a costume? Was he a performer? Where did he find these clothes? As he walked by, I felt not nervous, there was present a cold air and the smell of horses. He looked right into my eyes and I have felt embarrassment, but not in my eyes. I was shocked. There were no distortions at all like the ones I find in the others. No dismay at all. No chaos at all. He could look without his eyes!

October 18th, 1751. Same day

He walked slowly by us. And as he walked his legs strived and his foot touches the ground neatly. And he smiles at the Doctor. I have smiled before but why did I feel inflicted? He began to talk to the doctor, but why did thc doctor look at me? Were they talking about me? He nods his head and so does the man but are they nodding at me? I felt so distracted to leave but I couldn't do so. So I forced my body to stay. But I will go around the door where they cannot see, and I will listen. My plan will work this time! Dreaded! They cannot see me but I cannot hear them. Such a stupid plan it was. I left my hiding place. The doctor looks at me suspiciously. Was I doomed? I walked the other way, and watched his eyes turn away. What a fool I am. Why did I act this way? Of course the conversation is not about me. What a relief to discover this. The doctor looks again madly, so I left the circle and went up the hallway where he couldn't see me. What relief there was when I reached the end? But only to look beyond a window to look at what I will never have, or see. As the man left he put on a hat that I thought was a bag. It was almost a square shape. What oddity there must be out side? And then he looked at me so sternly and laughed. But why was I not puzzled?

October 18th 1751 Same Day

I returned to my room half wondering and half pondering. Wondering of the world outside, and pondering the things I have learned through this man. As I reached my chair I looked for my depressions. But instead I found a small and cozy hide away. It was one where I could dream about the things I don't have. I even have a chance to slowly learn about the outside through this friend of the doctor's. My favorite book and my writing paper is all I choose for now. I will learn from him and this will break at least my curiosity. Anyhow, I have been here long enough to be content with the little things I have; the hallways to ponder; the smoking room with an ashtray; my room to be alone; and myself to learn about. The plain-clothes man will be my teacher. I will buy books and read them at all times. And when the plain-clothes man comes I will be accurately alert at all times as if not to miss a single thing. I may be Looney and locked away, but that won't stop me. I am glad I picked Yahweh. He has given me the perfect ideas. The Devil may have given me things to play with. But Yahweh has given me my purpose, and I will stay with him.

October 20th, 1751

The daytime I spend eating and bathing. But it is at night near the lamplight in the darkness that I do my Learning. My eyes are more accurate and my mind (loves this.) The moon is my friend as it watches over my shoulders. And the coolness from the open window is my calmness. It also keeps me awake. This is a most appreciated decision since at night there is no noise from the others. And the doctor, the fool, has let me smoke in my room now. The only time I spend time as a day mouse is to watch things that are important. I love to watch the doctor. And when I write about him at night I feel that I have gotten back at him for all his foolishness. I even smile at him when he walks by. He only moves his eyes at me in return. But this is most humorous because he has no idea of the decisions I have been making. One day I will write a whole book! And he will not even know that I know how to write. Maybe he should check the books I bring into my room to study. I study so efficiently now that I could probably learn of his lessons. And I will make my own decisions!

October 22nd, 1751

It is as if I had drawn a cancer from somewhere at the height of my new life. It began as just a cold so I ignored it calmly. With all my disciplines intact, how could relapse become was my question. But it somehow germinated while I had no clue as to how. Why was I to suffer from a stressor? I have even seen the doctor try to remove it through a basic episode. Every time he is polite, I relax. Every time he demands something of me, I feel as if his decisions begin again. So when the latter happens, I go to my room and basically smile, and it is then gone. But then it returns farther. What is it? I ask myself each time. I know! I know now! It is leaving. It is not my disease coming, so it must be going. If I can reach my disease I can do anything. And then I can choose which of the others I will help. And I will make the doctor a fool. Now I know why the plain clothed man is always jeering at me. For to feel this way makes me want to jeer! And now I know why the doctor loves to use my decisions. I would love to one day use his. I know that this could be inborn. If I have inborn intelligence I could. And this would feel ecstasy again. I will jeer and jeer and no one will jeer back. And the doctor will look at me in astonishment. And I will jeer and return to my room and laugh. And I will choose other patients to teach! And maybe the doctor will not even know that it is I!

October 23, 1751

Today when I went to the dining hall for my breakfast the doctor caught my eye. I hoped by thinking that he looked because I had not been for breakfast the two days before. But as I gathered my choices to eat, I had s stubborn, short complex that he knew something. Instead of me watching him, he was studying me. Then intense emotion hit me as he nodded his head right at mine. I thought right away as though I was once again restricted. My eyes fell before his. But this time, actually, I showed to him a challenge, even though it was behind my worry. Then he nodded at my food, and minutes later he left the room. I could not help but to laugh at him and what he did. I laughed like a madman. I continued in hysterics until the whole room was at my attention. But I had to laugh again because they were so incompetent and I had been using them. Then I nodded my head at them just like the doctor did to me. Then I finished breakfast and returned to my room to sleep. Tonight I will learn how not to be so obvious. And I will learn precisely what to do at each angle he looks at me. He will never find out that I am leaning. Although if he did find out, the consequences would be barbaric. But that only makes the whole ordeal that much more fun.

November 12, 1751

What is this? I thought for long periods and as I look back I realize how infantile I really was. Now I know why the plain clothed man called me at the door. I love the feeling of strong decisions. My eyes are almost as wide as the doctors. But the game is what I enjoy. He doesn't even know how wide my eyes are. Here comes the premonition again, I laugh! No I am not afraid. Is it you? Is it the phantom doctor? Let us see! There are the phantom doctor's eyes. Goodbye phantom doctor. He must think I am a fool. Are none of you alive? Look at his eyes. If I tell them to look at his eyes I will win. And as long as he thinks I am afraid, and he cannot know I have learned, he will never know the truth. As long as I allow enough of my thoughts at night, he will never know. I remember seeing him and his tables as a God. Now, the tables are only in the other room. The only thing he knows is that my looks of fear have slightly diminished. And even when I smile he doesn't know because he is stupid enough to think he knows the truth. And as I sit in this dark room and ponder all these new experiences, I can remember when I didn't even know my name.

November 13, 1751

Today I sat right before my God. I was ready to discover exactly what he knew of myself. I was too brave. I sat in front of him as I had for years. And he startled me notoriously. As he lifted his head ever so slightly, he glared right into mine. It was the most powerful I have ever seen, even in his. Then he was immediate and abrupt with all things he did. I felt an impulse. I tried to relax. But as soon as I reached for my own mind, he looked straight into my eyes. Suddenly I stopped. Everything stopped and stayed in place, mostly my eyes. Then the fear subsided and I watched him look at me. And then the most fulfilling experience derived. I smiled into his glare. And I asked him what was his day like. And when my body looked like his, I dropped the posture. I acted like I always did. And my mind anticipated returning to my room to triumph. I showed him no satisfaction, remembering the days when I wished for it. And even as I remembered, he didn't even know. I thought, just to myself, if the whole occasion was in my mind. Maybe he didn't even look. But as he scribbled a notion on his paper, I knew he had.

November 15, 1751

Then I became the smarter one. All the letters I write are not just as they seem. You see the words I use can amuse my mind for hours. The words make me stronger, more content and even more intelligent. And the doctor thinks I am only writing to my friend. Although a friend I have never had. My companion is my self and no other. But for now that is all I need or want. My pencil is my guide, and as every day goes by, it feels more and more like the doctor's hand. I cross my legs, sit up right and smile ingeniously. It seemed as though I was the doctor. Then came a strangest feeling. I t was an anger that irrupted the devil in my soul. I tried to ignore it because Yahweh has promised me salvation. If I work with Yahweh in my vengeance, I could then use my anger constructively. The doctor is now my victim. Suddenly all frustrations began to surface. I could hear him walking down the hall. As I listened, I became alarmed and alert. My fantasy was to bring him down and win.

November 17, 1751

After a long night of thinking and planning, I awoke to a new day. I put on my robe and walked into the hall. The strangest coldness took me over. But I only let it go, as the heat was not on. But as I walked on my feet began to seem as though they were heavy. My toes were clenched into my slippers, and my toenails were felt in the tip of my shoe. As I went on the doctor came out of a room. He looked at me slyly, as if I were a woman. As I walked on behind him, I could not help but to notice the manner in which he traveled. Heal came first, then sole, then toe. The whole step was flowing and sort of attractive. My foot became so clenched that I began to limp. And to make the matter worse, I suddenly began to drag my left foot. My arms were even strange. I felt almost as if I was following him down the hall like a leper being led. Then I looked at his entire body. It was heavy! The feeling was horrible. I had never noticed, and it felt like a smack in my face. I had no heaviness. As I looked at the others minutes later, I almost wished that I were one of them. And as I looked upon a woman's eyes staring dumbly at mine, I couldn't help but to feel jealous.

November 20. 1751

With hands at my sides, and feet directly in front of me as I sit, all that I could do is listen to no thought. A woman sits near by moving forward and back, forward and back, and all I could do still is listen to no thought. The doctor entered with a long book and marked two times and then he left. And as I thought about his action, all that I could think of was a pen and a book. Again came the anger. Again were the frustrations. My eyes sped and sped to find that moment of my ingenious. But all I received was my stiffness. Then it left, and then it came back. But how was this? How did I become scornful? Why did I become abnormal again? Now his logic was beyond my understanding. What happened to that feeling like the doctor's? I lay my head in my hands, just to search for that single concept. Courage. Courage I thought. But what is courage without that concept. I was lost. I had lost every thought that I had. I could not even think that if I waited something would happen. All I worked for, I thought. But not even that could bring back the words. And still she moved back and forth. I felt almost as if I was helping her. I slightly jolted. And then I began to think again.

November 22, 1751

I went to my room. I held my pen. It was precise. The paper was indulging. My feet stretched like a birds. I crossed my legs. I felt to raise my arm in victory. But instead I clenched it and shake. They were the evil. I knew this now. Then my mind swooned. The clutching, the tension was gone. But what if it returned? I was devastated. I felt the pen. I felt the paper. I felt the concepts again! I thought to draw circles and lines. I thought to draw shapes. I thought to interpret anything that came to my mind. Creativity isn't logical. The things in my room circled around me. They waited for my creativity. Then my arms were rigid. They were light, but they were stronger. I thought of the doctor and how he didn't know. Then silliness came to mind. But what would guide my thoughts. Nothing, I thought. Nothing would guide my thoughts!

November 24, 1751

I sat in the corner of my unit with pen and pencil in hand, and looked out the window at the fields. For one short moment, I pondered on what to write. But this was soon interrupted by the need to draw. Suddenly a need for the arts came to mind, and the feeling was very inspiring. But I could not think of what to draw. Then, as if God had sent, the plain clothed man appeared at the entrance of the room. He had grown a mustache, and this was very humorous to me, since my plan was next to try and draw him. Very conveniently, he sat at a table with the doctor almost completely across from myself. First were minutes of curves and lines, until I began to graciously connect them into images. With perceptual precision, I drew the hat, the arms of the coat, and a black boot with light upon it. At the same time I became courageous and ultimately impressed with my talent. The figure was in length of six inches. I had even and almost completed a gun, which I did not see. The feeling was robust since again I had found an innate intelligence. This I will love to work with. I wrote the title, "The Man From Outside."

December 1, 1752

Today comes another winter, with snow falling through gusts of wind.

But this will be my first to watch with my new intelligence. The winds came out like songs from a woodwind. They channeled in different directions like the bow, and the sounds would flourish. This I enjoyed, so I wrote it down in this diary. Last winter, all that I could do was stare. I could not feel the power of the winds gusting, and the snow falling everywhere. It was a blizzard out there, and I was nice and cozy inside.

It made me wonder if the experiences I have had in this institute are like the ones other people have outside. As I looked I imagined angers and tensions. I saw poor people and rich people. Maybe the rich people had too much. Maybe the poor people didn't. They wore black and white, just as we do in here. The doctor came to mind, and as he did he had circles under his eyes. Mine had none. Maybe this is God's answer. Maybe the whole world has experienced just as much pain as I. I watched the gusty winds drive the snow in any direction it wanted. For the first time I wondered if, besides the others, that maybe I was not alone.

December 3, 1751

The snow has accumulated for two days now. As I stare outside before lunch, everything was covered with snow. As I looked out the day hall window, I could feel the heat from the fireplace, and I drank hot tea. The atmosphere was warm and cozy. The room was not crowded, and was unusually silent. Suddenly I noticed that the teacup felt very dirty, and at the same time, so did my hand. Then, as I concentrated on my arms, they also felt unusually dirty. I went to the washroom to put some soap to my hands and arms. After several tries, nothing changed. My arms and hands felt contaminated. Then I remembered the feeling from before my intelligence. It had stopped and then came back. And the contamination would mean I am ill. Then the atmosphere seemed to have filminess about it. The air around my head was lighter. The talking in the room was quieter. Through all this my mind was clear and the contamination was partly dry. My intelligence had no idea what this was. Then, in came the doctor. Quizzically, I wondered if in some way I could try to understand this part. I could ask the doctor, but he would think that I should be treated. This is obviously not what I needed. Contamination, thin air, silence, these occurrences sound like a working of the mind. But was it a clear mind or an ill mind? Could I actually be getting better? Could intelligence cause normality? Am I not just an abnormal psychopath?

December 5, 1751

I sat quietly in the day hall trying to ignore this annoying feeling. But all I could do is concentrate on it. Then, the same concentrations began to direct me to other things in the room. I became very irritable. Then come these cravings. I needed to drink or eat, or do something to relieve myself. I drank coffee, and as I did the soothing was as I have never felt from the drink. As I looked upon the objects that I need to concentrate on, I first needed to change them. The objects on the table I needed to arrange. Then I began to protect them. They became small people in my mind. Then came back my intelligence and happiness.

Then come the doctor again. The usual feeling of guilt and fear came upon me. But to my surprise, it cleared from my thoughts. How could such a strange feeling accompany a clear thought? I must find the answer! But wait! My eyes are connected. They are both looking at the doctor. I turned my attention to the objects. Then I sat and protected them with my eyes on the doctor. He had no idea that I was. Then I began to concentrate much clearer. Then I thought of washing my hands. I looked to the doctor and then smiled. I went to the washroom and washed my hands. I decided that I would do this every day, several times. And the to objects I would pay close attention.

December 7, 1751

Today, as always, I went to he washroom to clean my arms and hands. Then I went to the dinning room for breakfast. I will also wash afterwards, and then read by the window in the hall. As I left the washroom, the doctor came by. He looked at me puzzled. I could not help but laugh. It was so humorous, that I giggled and smiled. He asked me how I was doing with an enlightened smile. Again I laughed. It almost seemed as though he knew the way I felt. For the first time, I felt good about my abnormalities. Was this winning? I felt it was. And as he walked down the hall, I followed close behind watching every move and gesture. For once his actions I enjoyed. He turned and smiled and laughed. I felt almost to skip and make a scene.

Then, as I watched him, I remembered my old states. But this time I did not fret. I thought of a return. Just to see what the feelings are like. This I would do tonight.

Maybe abnormality is a common state, something not to be feared. And as I looked at the doctor, he looked back, and slowly turned his head away. As I entered the dinning room, I felt a joy. Then an excitement arose.

December 9, 1751

The late afternoon was satisfactory. I thought of maybe what the wines were like. What the women were like. I excused myself from God. I was only trying to enjoy the feelings, and not as a sin. My arms came around the chair arms, and legs relaxed. Then a feeling came to mind. First I hesitate, but I let it go. They would never know. So I looked around and watched them. Some were sitting forward.

Most were sitting uncomfortably. Most seemed completely dismayed. The feeling was just as dismantling. I searched the room for attention. Then I allowed the emotion. It would be a new emotion and I was anticipating. It must feel good. As I allowed it I made my discovery. It was the way I felt before. I remembered the table and the birds with the guiding. Then it was so painful. But now, it felt so good.

Enlightened, I left the room to be alone. Night was coming. So as usual, I will go to my room.

December 10, 1751

This morning, though I chose not to depress who ever may have found my diary, I have become slightly paranoid. As I entered the day hall, I found one of the more comfortable chairs empty. It was one that supports all of the posture. I sat in it to watch the others play a game with one of the staff. As I pondered, I took notice to my arms and hands, and then to my legs and feet. At that time a thought came to mind. What if there is no God of goodness, but a mad evil genius who is portraying himself as a God. Then there would be absolutely nothing to trust. I have had thoughts such as this, paranoid thoughts. This one was not insanity, but a repetitive, recurring thought that I could not exclude from my thinking. If my creator was a mad genius, how can I be sure that what I see and sense, in sight or hearing, is not a world of deception? First death became upon me. Then what am I to do with no God once again? Then a very esteemed thinking came to mind. I, who was earlier lesser, can now confide in himself without worrying about my God! But what a bore it is to be crazy, again the thought came to mind and for hours I could not knock it. What if everything positive is a deception? Then the doctor would be fooled! The nurses would be fooled! Even the plain clothed man and all his friends would be fooled!

God! I wish I could control my thoughts better!

December 12, 1751

Today I sat and sipped tea and smoked a cigar I received from my friend Marco. But where he received the smoke I will never know. I saw him smoking and asked where he had found the smoke and he merely handed me a cigar and then told me to go away. With this I still feel the laughter in my tongue. So I sat very well relaxed and watched the others. Then a most absurd thought came to my head. I had never truly known the name of this institution of which I live. A.M.P was the only name I have known. But what could it stand for. I contemplated the stone walls and wondered how aged the room is. Then I wondered about other people before my time who were ill. I have heard about cages and chains. As I contemplated I almost felt that I was lucky. I began to imagine the plain clothed man, and rationally claimed that even he was not as content as I. For some reason my eyes could not discontinue watching movements. Suddenly, in the corner of my eyes, came Marco. He came to sit with me. In a timely discussion, I mentioned the name of our institution. He told me the name. It was the Alliance for the Mentally Poor.

December 14, 1751

You're mentally poor. You're mentally poor. On and on I have repeated these thoughts in my head. But the grim smile of satisfaction on my lips would not go away. Thinking of the plain clothed man, I had almost begun to laugh. As I thought of the icon of mental illness, I almost had an insight. The icon is a man in complete laughter. My insight was into what the man was laughing at, or why? Maybe he himself had the same feeling as I. They call it manic episodes. But is this the truth? Is this reality? Or is it just something that the doctors have contemplated. Are they correct? Is there something within myself other than illnesses that makes he have a sense of eruptive pride. I could stay and sip, smoke, and dream all day. Who wants to be the plain clothed man, or the doctor? Not I! Is it not possible that the words "Alliance for the Mentally Poor," only mean poor in the sense of money?

December 16, 1751

Again I sat and smoked. The laughter almost erupted this time. But this time it was not confidence. This time it was because of the objects I stole from the doctor's coat. I scanned the room to be sure that no one who could convict me was anywhere in the room. As minutes passed I was sure. Then I brought them from my pocket. They were a few English coins. My fingers were very stiff as I held and observed them. Never have I seen a coin. I again scanned the room, and nobody was there. So at the table I sat and studied, with the coins set out on the surface. Eventually my ignorance passed, though rather timely, as is usual when I learn something new. The size of my nose and the stiffness in my lips concluded as I stared with amazement. On the coins were some writings, and of this I knew. I also recognized the pictures. But dreams of intuition excited me as I wondered of how one uses them. How much money was there before my eyes? *May I pay for a woman? May I please buy this horse? Than you!* I dreamed of how I could spend money! But strangely, this was enough.

December 17, 1751

Immediately I replaced the coins into by pocket because the doctor had returned to the room. My curiosity ran wild, so I returned to my room to examine the coins. I locked my door in opposition to the doctor's rule, of which I had no concord. I pulled the chair to my little desk and set the coins out on the surface. Some were gold, some silver, larger, or smaller. I guessed that this symbolized the amount one could by with each coin. Before me were ten pieces. Three had the number 10 written on it, three had the number 5, two had the number 25, and the last one had the number 50. Of course the person who had a coin with the number 50 could buy more than the person with number 25. And if I had two coins with number 25, I could buy just as much as a person with a number 50 coin. Then a sudden feeling erupted as my fingers touch several coins. I have money that I stole from the doctor's pocket. Steeling is a crime, and I could be under arrest. I gathered the coins, and moved outside my room with the objective of returning the coins to the doctor's coat.

December 17, 1751 (cont.)

I walked near the doctor's office. I stalked by several times impatiently. He sat at his desk with his coat hung out on the back of his chair. He looked at me. My eyes almost begged. I was nervous, horrified. I could tell he knew I was. The back of my legs became immediate and sturdy. I couldn't stop checking his face. My left leg began to shake. As I tried to walk away, the nurses began to laugh. Once again, yet once long ago, God came to mind. All that I could hold onto was that God could, and would, save me. I looked at my door, and then at the laughing nurses. I went to my room and closed the door. I waited. I sat on my cot with my hands on my head.

There was only one thing to do. I went to the door of the office and threw the coins onto his table. I then left quickly, begging that they would not put me under arrest.

Again I sat in my room and waited. A half an hour went by, and no one came. I lie in my room and sleep for hours relieved.

December 19, 1751

I awoke to a dreary morning. It was cold and foggy. I sat for breakfast, and was unusually hungry this day. There was a slight mumbling sound, and clicking dishes. Suddenly, the doctor entered the room. The monitors and nurses rose in the back of the room. The doctor took his place in the front, facing all of the patients. After his announcement, I was left astonished. I was in shock. Every one was appalled. There were whispers and looking, and even pointing. My eyes dropped to the table. I didn't know whether to be thankful. *Shall it be good?* I asked myself. *Shall I be devastated?* The doctor was to leave to go elsewhere. A sharpness came to my mind as I wondered what might happen to me if a new doctor would come. Oddly, the man, whom I once despised and feared, is now cherished and needed. I have never had another doctor!

January 1, 1752

The horn sounded, so I immediately rose to my feet and changed into my new clothes. I fumbled with the doorknob nervously, and it finally opened. I stood before my room door and waited. I watched as everyone did the same as I. Then the line of nurses walked the hall, from end to beginning, and checked us. We had just finished our noon meal. Then came the torture, the chains. Walking in them gave neither my arms nor my legs room to move. We left the institution, walking a mile to a large area with muddy dirty water. Every now and then a horse or carriage would ride by. I could tell by the eyes of the doctor that this was meant to demean me. But the same old laughter and confidences were still inside me. As we walked down the narrow paths, some steep some stable, I watched the beautiful trees and grass. I almost licked at the dewdrops in the misty air. Once I made the gesture and had to laugh as everyone starred. I must laugh at the expression on the doctor's face as I am supposed to give in. I even have a trick. I can skip with my chains on. When I did this I had a laugh from the aides. When the carriages pass, I wave my hands and say good day. The most appalling thing happens! They never smile. I could even bare a new doctor!

Chapter Two

Excerpt From Iccabod and the Dragon Slayer

By Susan Cane

Driving through paths of dirt road and fresh country air in my vehicle, the grossness of the dirty air and pollution sickened me. I was on my way to a new institute. I was assigned to new cases, and these were not my first. The demented were an eerie sort. It seems that the strictest discipline does not encounter any prognosis to cease. Continuous bathing, grooming and feeding are the basics. But recently many theories have developed. Though some institutions do not agree, many have been left from their boxes and chains. Contemporarily, such treatments to me seem like torture. These are replacing exorcisms, and it seems that something will take these methods of treatment away from the churches.

Through my own experiences, this institute to me seemed like a prison. Surrounded by practically nothing, there were bars on windows and gates flanking the entire estate. Appalled, I watched as a man appeared at a top window with restraints around his arms. He watched as I led my horses and entered the building. The same man appeared at the door, watching every thing I did as I moved on. I don't mean to offend him or anyone, but I was in complete fear.

I entered the halls, only to find a repetitive chant. "Iccabod!" Would be sent at one time. At another, while passing by a woman, "Iccabod!" One man came down the hallway revealing the word," Iccabod!" I passed the event as demented.

Before reporting myself, I decided to explore the facilities. I wanted to find any boxes or rooms with chains. Sure enough, I found my first clue. There was a trapdoor. I checked my surroundings, and curiously opened the door to find many stares. They were steep and spiral. I went in. The odor was too much. I pulled a handkerchief from my coat pocket, held it to my nose, and continued down the stares. If not for a single flame, I would not have seen it. A man, very small, sat on the floor looking at me. The room must not have been smaller than an animal cage. So there I stood, with him just watching me. I had no comment to make to him. I merely turned away, and proceeded to leave.

"You know Iccabod?" He interrupted me. I turned to look. "You'll know Iccabod." He continued. Quietly I continued up the stares. As I reached the top, he began again, "You know Iccabob?"

I closed the door, but was startled as I stopped before a man. He introduced himself, "I'm Iccabod." Then he left.

I vigorously brushed the dust from my clothes, as the chamber was not cleaned or attended to keeping. I conspicuously turned to watch the man who had identified himself as Iccabod. He was a very short and small man dressed in a large white straight jacket. He seemed to be merely wondering the halls as if everything was normal.

I had just sat to drink my coffee, when a man came in and introduced himself. "My name is Dr. Allen Stooks. I'll be your assistant." We shook hands.

After him came a man, much shorter, who was carrying a large stack of papers. He dropped the heavy bundle on my desktop, and left. "What are these?" I dumbly asked. "These are the records of all patients in this institution," the doctor replied. I want for you to read them.

I remembered Iccabod and the others. My curiosity was so high that I had to ask the question. "Who is Iccabod? I met him today?"

The doctor seemed very uncomfortable. "Iccabod has been here quite a while. He is deaf and dumb, yet oddly reports grandiose hallucinations and voices. He's probably the worst here," the doctor replied.

For the next few moments the voice and words of the doctor left my attention. I remembered Iccabod. In my thoughts he was wandering the halls, looking out windows, wearing straight jackets, and maybe calling out. I knew by my inspirations that there was something unique about Iccabod, and that I would find it, and change him completely. I gestured to the doctor and nodded my head, and went off to a deep dream about discovering the world of Iccabod.

As I walk the halls trying to rid of my being a stranger, I entered the largest room and explored. Two patients sat together as one nodded at the other, and they both looked at me. Both began to laugh.

"What? I asked. "What are you laughing at?"

"Iccabod." One patient replied. "Iccabod called you the next dragon slayer."

Suddenly, Iccabod entered the room and gestured franticly through sign language to the others. Of, course they laughed again. And I was left in complete wonder. I assured myself that brushing up on my sign language would be the best start.

Reading reports on Iccobob was very enlightening. My dreams are coming true. A deaf man listening to voices can write. A man born deaf walks around a hospital in a restraint looks at me positively. *Restraints! Restraints!* I thought to myself while trying to find the doctors notes. *Why restraints?* I found them. It was discipline. My hands left the papers as I looked at them. They were kind hands. They were humane hands. They were hands that wanted to remove Iccabod's restrictions.

Days past as most of my work went towards Iccabod. One day, as my inconvenient assistant was not present, I asked Iccabod into my office. He began to franticly move back and forth with an angry glare. "Why do you think you are in restraints, Iccabod?" I asked him politely. He gave me no answer except for an expression of disgust. "Can I trust you if I take them off of you?" I inquired again.

Moments passed as I stood up from my seat and approached him. I began to remove the restrictions, while smiling joyfully at his surprised expression. Then he erupted. Angry fists of demented rage poured at my face leaving me practically unconscious on the floor. He ran out of the room. I stood up immediately and chased him. I was relieved to find the nurses holding him down and returning the restraints. I dropped to a chair exhausted and astonished. Never would I remove Iccabod's restraints again. My head went to my hand in failure. I returned my attention to him, only to find him grinning at me in victory.

That evening, I decided to brush up on my sign language. I borrowed a book from the library, and sat comfortably with most of my attention on the signs. Repetitive memories of school passed through my mind. Memories of learning temperaments, disturbances, and nifty tools like sign language. Luckily, it didn't seem new to me. It was not lost, or distorted. With a touch of motivation, I held my right hand up and began using signs. I spelled the words "help," "talk" and then "come with me." Then I turned to emotional and subjective words like "love," "happy" and "need." As premises poured in I began to create sentences, and then paragraphs. I was almost ready to face Iccabod, and communicate with him.

After hours passed, I closed the book in excitement. I was ready to face Iccabod and communicate. Finding him was the first problem I took on. How could one man not be seen in such a small environment? I went into the largest room once again, only to hear the fable remark. "Iccabod!" Was gestured to me, again with laughter.

"Where is Iccabod?" I replied with a sense of their own humor. "I can't find him anywhere." Several patients seemed to be looking in a direction right behind my shoulder. One points in this direction. "He's right there." I turned surprisingly to find him there, with less space between our faces than what is supposed by our culture.

"Iccabod!" I said, not remembering his handicap. "Oh, sorry", I admitted.

I then began the signs. I began with, "My name is Rubenstein. I am your doctor."

Astonishingly, he replied. "I hate doctors." Was signed before my eyes.

Then was the moment of surprise. He slowly spat out "I hate all doctors." Then he turned and left. I let him go.

I searched the room for faces. I was seeking anyone that may seem to be different from the expressions I have been receiving, especially from Iccabod.

But all I saw were angry expressions of disgust, impatience, and maybe one-day revenge. I left the room feeling a strange pain in my heart, one of which no one really cared. With an idea, I became motivated. My goal would be to change their emotions. I would not punish them. I would treat them, and help them.

One night went by as I was again sitting in my office, contemplating about how to win their hearts. They are not my patients. They are people who are sick. They need help, not chains and cages. I thought that maybe sitting with them in a group might strengthen the road to my objective of becoming a friend. This has been done before.

One good thing did go right. Most of the patients were in the large room, which the hospital called the day hall. I walked in with a newspaper, called "The Wildly."

I announced my intentions to the entire room. "Things have changed," I began. "Today we are going to read about the news." I received a dumb stare.

"Who wants to know what's going on in the real world?" I asked.

Suddenly, as if hidden by camouflage, Iccabod raced towards me. With the restraints not worn, he signed before my eyes again in anger. He signed, "I'd rather go to the room than read your news." He left the day hall in a frenzy. Again I let him go, and left the hall like dog with a tail between its legs.

Hours go by before I recalled that I had left my newspaper in the day hall. I stood up only to find a situation that was beginning to burden me. My legs were much to big being under the desk and I consistently had to squeeze myself out to stand up. A small feeling of irritation began. I walked towards the hall, only to find five patients sitting with the paper, each with a pencil in their hand. There were numerous drawings on the paper. I had to take a deep breath to hold back my frustration. I walked to the desk, grabbed and sorted the pages, and left in a slight rage, only to be laughed at once again.

I returned to my desk and lye the papers out on its surface. On the first page was a picture of a man who was reported as a doctor much like myself. Of course the picture had common scribbling on it such as a mustache, thick eyebrows and a small beard on his chin. I myself found it to be rather amusing. I read the heading allowed. "First Sector of Research on the Mentally Ill. Read of the recent findings of Sigmund Freud." I had recalled reports on this man's writings, but have often discarded him as gibberish.

The next day, after sleeping in my quarters, I noticed that my office could use a little cleaning. So I began moving boxes and sorting papers. As a small amount of time passed, I found several music boxes. A genuine idea came to mind. Music could be a way of breaking the ice. It may even be possible to use it as a treatment. I found a patient, unfortunately not Iccabod, lying on a bed in her room. She seemed to be very uncomfortable, as she was holding her arms in sort of a statue. I set the music box on her night table and let it play. I watched for just one moment. Then the most illuminating thing happened. She nodded at me. I left her alone, and planned to return later.

Hours went by with my trying to be patient, and allow some sort of effect.

But my curiosity ran wild, and I left my office and returned to her room. But this time I found not statue positions, but movement. There was movement of her arms around the top of her head, then to the sides, and finally stretching out around her shoulders. Even though the situation seemed very demented, my victory was honored, as the arm movements seemed to be with the music. As I stared in disbelief, the movements became very choppy, as if she was trying to show me something. But I left her alone once I received the all to common glare of disgust. My insecurities were haunting me.

I sat in my office for hours, just going through everyone's files. Finally I picked up Iccabod's reports. Suddenly he appeared at my office door. He made statue like movements in front of me, and then shook his fist. I assumed he was angry at my treating someone else.

Reading my patient reports, as it was daybreak, I heard the sound of a patient calling out. Annoyed by the interruption, I once again left the office to find what was wrong. It was Iccabod. His restraints were removed, and he with another patient were fighting on the floor, along with the nurses.

"What is going on!?" I demanded to know. "That is my patient, and I want to know how those restraints were lifted." Replying to my question, Iccabod turned to look at me, restrained by the large arms of Mocco, a male nurse. He was carried away.

Again I demanded. "How were the restraints lifted?"

Mocco Replied, "The other patient removed them doctor."

My shoulders slumped as I realized what I had done. I had yelled at Icabob.

My love for him ached in my heart. Tonight he will be in seclusion, and I will have to try to sleep.

I was so very relieved the next morning when I found out Iccabod was finally released from his isolation. But the horrifying gloom that struck when he looked into my eyes was sinful. My eyes cried out desperately. His turned away in indecision. My shoulders slumped, realizing how hurt I really was.

The other doctor was the next to appear at the door. I welcomed him.

He seemed very disturbed. His next question gave me an endearing enlightenment.

He gave to me an assignment. I was to work with Iccabod. No rules, and no regulations between us. The question is, what to do?

So I entered the storming world of Iccabod. The world of restraints, moping silence, and small words. It was a world of hallucinations, voices and paranoiacs.

But there was a bridge, an iron, obelisk bride between us. It was a bridge called the doctor, or in his own words, the dragon slayer. In small words I must break this bridge. The first words must be I love you.

Chapter Three

The Melancholy Maid

By Susan M Cane

This place was soft and so tranquil at last there was time to relax and not experience anxiety. The arms were at the side, and legs were drawn out and lightly comfortable. There were no annoying auditory or phantom distractions. Silence was still and burdenless. There were no sights or feelings of death. There were no reasons, entirely, to feel cold.

The room was so vivid and distorted, and eyesight seemed very unfocused. Suddenly a figure appears in and was surprising. He seemed vaguely familiar. He said, "Hi Momma!" The feeling was startling and abrupt. "Who are you?" Was asked in complete wonder. He replied, "It's Julian, your son." The chill was cold and bare, almost blunt. A yearning came out almost into an odor. Utterly, and of course, there was crying. Not just a slight one, but very heavy. "Julian, you found me!" Was beckoned. He smiled and gaily nodded his head. Brightness never felt poured through the eyes as if it was forced, and then there was salvation.

But it was needed to embrace her only son. *But, there was no movement.* Was thought of. "How did you find me here?" Was asked. Still no there was no movement. There was trying, but it was as though there was displacement or disassociation. "Come to me Julian! Come here to your Mother." There was begging. Arms were feminine and heavy. Hair was gray and curly.

Helplessness was activating. Help was needed. Reacting was needed, but there couldn't be. "I'm a cripple." Was cried out. "I'm a cripple. There is nothing I can do, Julian."

Suddenly, a foreign noise was heard. It wasn't known at first. But soon it was known! It was known as before! "Not again," was said. The whole scene was fading and there was complete shock. "Lucy!" The voice said. "Get up!" Then the main bell was rung.

Eyes were staring with painful prosecutions. There was to be eating and bathing, and today washing hair. Hair was too thin to comb it. A brown rag dress was chosen to wear. "I like this one," was said out loud to the self. Things to be done would be done in the usual way. The physical pains were unbearable. Mental anguishes were notorious. There was to be no prejudice anger. There would be no son to hold or see again. Any crying would be allowed, but discipline would be in the same way. Treatments would continue all day. Then the Doctor would leave and the old maid could sleep again.

Dinner was eaten, the day done. Showers were recorded, and then time was free. Smoking was obsessive for hours. One cigarette, than two, than three, on and on, there was smoking. A long flannel gown was worn, and nicotine stains were on fingers. Hair was done in curlers, gray, thin, and slightly wet. Hours go by, and there was standing and going to bed.

Window half open, blankets were drawn and the lights were turned out. Body was turned to the right, and shoulders curled. Lips were licked, and eyes were closed. Knuckles were gripped onto the seams of the blankets. Hours go by, and there was finally relaxation.

Eyes opened, and there was Julian with open arms. "Julian, come to your mother" was suggested.

But Julian stood still. His face did not move. The picture became frozen. It was still and motionless. Then her arms and body could not move.

Chapter Four

Food

By Susan M Cane

The air was as cold as her steps on the rock hard, cement pavement, especially with her shoes being wet from sleeping in the subway tunnel that night. It was just as cold as the ache in her head. The memories would not subside this night. Every time her eyes met another's, sometimes searching for some sort of answer, there was either a blank stare or a passive glance. While inside her head, memories were emerging. Memories were as unsatisfying and at worst not soothing. It seemed like two distinct dimensions where hers was a horror, and theirs would walk home. At all this time, she was searching for some place to live.

It was not only a place to rest and eat, but also a need for medication and mental attention. She could receive attention from the state institute, but she would rather drudge through the cold weather in order to find any small sort of haven. Her worries were whether she would have to sleep in the streets tonight.

She wanted to turn off to the neighborhoods surrounding the worse parts of town, but that would only mean watching people live normal lives. It would be to look into windows and watch the family and children eat their supper, and discuss what happened that day. Here she could become cozy with the sight of demented eyes like her own.

When a man who seemed as though he had money walked by, he became very abrasive at the sight of their looking. He obviously lived in that different world, where the fireplaces and the hot tea were waiting. A place where the carpets were clean and warm, and the walls enclosed the man with heat insulating the whole room. Back in her world, the memories were whether to sleep in a place where the normal people went home at night. The word emergency was all repressed now.

The square unit in which she would sleep in tonight would be found soon enough. Newspapers would need to be found, dry newspapers. The air is to cold for the night. Hopefully she could sleep all night without being moved. Her bandana would be as reacted to as the park bench. The kind of scene you see in the media, only to be passively ignored while the mail is being opened from some far off place like Europe or never land. Maybe a letter from the federal or state government could help her.

But even the steps to the building would make anyone cringe and go another way. Who would want to take water from the wine cup? To her, it seems like a mountain with only cliffs and edges that go straight into the sky with no way to climb or reach the top. It would only to be stared at and to wonder why, and all in another world.

The large and thick green jacket was perfect for keeping her warm. The bandana was worn to keep the others away. The large boots were now full of holes that couldn't be patched. When another woman walks by, her boots drag and flop. She can still look around to find more confidence. Even though the bandana is gleamed at, it can still be her very own symbol. Her blue jeans were wide and dirty and covered most of her boots. Still the men on the street sometimes looked at her, only to get a bad look in return.

She wanted to be alone. There had to be some place around here where she could be alone. She dreamed it. It would be dark with only small animals and misty air. The thought was as dark as the night she saw. It would have to be. Any light would never bring the silence she needed. It would be a place where she could sit and dream. She would be taking out a cigarette and staring at the night. Her feet would be warmed in the pond, which was hot and warm. The birds would peacefully fly over in a dark blue sky. The trees surrounding her would be cold and cooling, with wetness in the leaves. After she slept, the sun would come up and she would stare at all the land around her, with no one there.

But here she was on the street with no place to go. These streets were not crowded. But the need to be alone was compulsive. The hunger pains made it worse. Where was she going to eat? The ache in her stomach went right to her head. "Medicine or something!" She says out loud. Then came the disgust.

Suddenly she saw a boy. He seemed at least under nine. He had the same dirty face and torn clothes with holes. She decided to approach the boy.

"Hey!" She exclaimed as he tried to push by her and through the crowd. She turns to watch him pass. "Hey kid, where are you going?"

The boy turns with a lost expression on his face. He just shakes his head and continues.

She thought of how dangerous things might get if she left him alone. So she caught up to him. "Stop!" She commanded. He turned to look at her, with the same lost expression. She smiled as she looked down. "Come on," she requested. He only looked up. "Come on," she repeated. So he turned and walked away with her.

His small feet also wore torn shoes and his face was thick with dirt.

He wore a leather jacket with a long tare on the right sleeve. The shoulders were bunched up because the jacket was too large. But he looked with a cold stare, and his mind wondered attentively as he walked by the strangers on the road. He walked with his hands in his pockets. She just looked down and smiled from the corner of her eye.

They walked quite a long while. Both were exchanging short stories of their lives on the street, his being only a few months. Her's had been quite a few years. As they momentarily passed different memories, the thought of where they would sleep tonight, and what they would eat, came to her mind. She had confidence in herself. She had been planning these problems for years now.

Suddenly, as they were walking along, a strange man stopped the boy. She was startled at first, but then relaxed as she realized the boy was familiar with the man.

"Hey Joey!" The man exclaimed. "You're away from home again?"

The boy seemed as though he was reluctant. "Yeah," Was his only reply.

Then the man offered to take him away. "Maybe you should come with me Joey, you need to sleep and eat."

The boy passed a sorrowful glance at her. He turned to the man and answered, "Okay." He went away with the man.

The woman watched a moment, and then proceeded to walk down the street, glancing profoundly at the world around her.

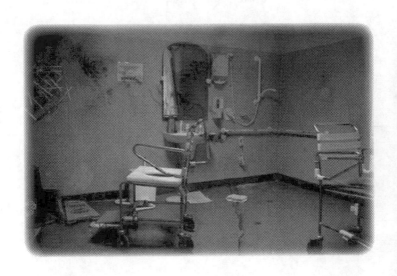

Chapter Five

Penny is Gone

It happened in a small room surrounded by four thick, stonewalls and a metal door. The room was extremely crowded, and the temperature was cold. Most of the people had been in this room for hours. There was some moaning, and at times there was the sound of footsteps, echoing with the sounds of the doctor. The quirky footsteps he uses with his long legs and his shouts and commands cause all to be dismal. Strange, it was all to be strange. Mentally challenged brains would listen.

Margaret was a patient here. Everyone watched as she began to hit her head on the wall. Then she began to hit it harder. She continued to hit her head until a stain was seen on the wall. Ryan, another schizophrenic, was returned from treatment. He was so exhausted from the practice that he could hardly stand.

He nearly collapsed as he searched the room for faces. Everyone knew what it was like to be treated. His eyes were staring upwards with absolutely no expression, and nobody could bear to watch him. Then came a woman with a stern face and broad shoulders. She didn't seem like the others. She seemed more rested. She sat gracefully onto the cold, rusted benches.

As Penny looked around, there were ghostly pale images. In the shadows, black and gray clothing was hidden, bringing out sights of distorted eyes and scenes of tortured and demented people. Still she seemed perched upon the cold metal furniture that was supposed to be used by them daily. She heard the doctor moving around the hospital and when she did she saw the sullen looks of the despair.

"Kill me!" Ryan began at her feet, "He gave Penny a hard and cold stare." "I don't want to live... here... any... more," Ryan spoke slowly. He almost seemed like the devil was in his look. His face was expressionless.

Penny comforted Ryan. "Shhh! Ryan, it's nice and cold in here. Don't worry, the room is nice and cold. I've been through this, too," she explained. She shook her head as she studied each patient.

Everyone was still very passive, but somehow Penny seemed as though she would stand out. It seemed as though there were barbaric treatments like blood letting of the brain with leeches. At other times' people were locked in tiny cages. And every time there was moaning and fearful faces as Dr. Erickson came into the room.

"Open this door here and now!" Dr. Erickson commanded the nurses. "I want to see my people," he demanded. "They had better be clean."

"I'll hose them doctor!" One assistant came to the door like a trained monkey.

"Just let me in," Erickson began. Erickson pointed his fingers, stamped his feet and jerked his arms in anticipation. "I want in!" He pointed his finger at his assistant and stamped his right foot in command. "This is my jurisdiction!"

Penny nodded her head, and she closely held Margaret. "Please, everyone should relax," she says. She tried to compose the others. "I know what to do." Everyone stared at her in disbelief.

She looked around the room and awaited the doctor's arrival. A face appeared around the door with a large sneer, clenched teeth and an evil grin. He studied each patient's situation and awaited his or her grim reactions. But Penny seemed too enlightened. The doctor was not influenced. He was too unabashed with his nature. But he secured his fashion with the slap of her face. After all, Penny was holding Margaret.

Penny's face only moved to the right. Her hand began to shake, but her eyes stared at him. His right elbow went upwards as he patted his chest in victory. The doctor loved his victory. Penny's eyes dropped. But she gave him a long, stern stare. Then he stamped his feet as he left the room. He turns and points to the nurses, and they leave with him.

Penny Prayed. She soothed them with words. "Why must our minds be the devil's? Why are our souls so taken? Please Jesus, perform an exorcism"

The leeches were agitated as Dr. Erickson removes each one, and he placed them on each side of Ryan's head. The blood seeped from Ryan's head as he lay face down on the table. He had been removed from the room for his bloodletting treatment.

"Write him up and tell the truth," the doctor requests." No matter how hard I bleed him he just will not respond." He taps his finger on the table. "That's all," he finishes. He sternly folded his arms and was astonished at how the nurse was not immediate with his suggestion.

Ryan was returned to the room after bloodletting. He returned to the floor at the foot of the benches.

Suddenly Penny sees a leech on Ryan's head that wasn't removed. Without any control, Penny begins to tremble. She throws Margaret from her lap and jolted. She falls to the floor and goes into seizures. The whole room stared in disbelief.

"Help me!" She screamed, "Help me! I'm having an attack. Somebody help me!" Penny was lying helplessly on the floor jolting and trembling. "Somebody get the doctor! I'm having an attack," she continued.

As Penny looked around the room, she saw that everyone was looking at her with the same expressionless faces as when she had arrived. Ryan came into the scene, and she saw him watch her like a child losing his mother. Then everything disappeared in her sight. In what seemed to be seconds, she woke and saw a cold and sinister room with every face like that of a stranger.

Someone entered from a metal door, surrounded by four walls of stone. "You three and you four over there," she says. She treats patients like cattle. "Get up! You have to have your treatments. This group follows me. You are going to see Father Myer."

This time Penny was taken out of the room. But she walked along with the others as if it were second nature. Then she saw him. It was to be the symbol of God. He wore the cross and the collar. But his face was quite the opposite. It had the same features of the reaper, just like everyone did. She felt no path to the paradise that was so promised by Father Myer's preaching. His face was the same cold stare.

Chapter Six

Killbird

by Susan M Cane

The building sat on a good-sized hill that looked straight down on acres of land. All around were trees that probably kissed the land for centuries. There were also the big black gates that surrounded the secluded spot. In particular spots were the half decent benches where the people who lived here liked to sit. They would sit and stare at the same red bricks in the tall building. At times you would see the people with white coats and plain clothes who would monitor the place.

Sarah entered through the two-way doors and hobbled to her favorite bench. Patients watched her the closest. Sarah was a senior, and she knew the best way to look. Sarah's eyes were always still at any way you looked at her.

The birds, on the small place before her, always invaded the spot as Sarah sat and thought. But the joy of her day would be when the blackbird would come and talk to her. "Are they still teasing you?" The bird would ask this of her often. "Yesterday you said they were tying you up in the restraints."

"Who them?" Sarah tended to deny things. "Those people know better than that!" She explained.

"They did it again," said the bird.

"Oh, It's not so bad," Sarah lied. Her eyes dropped to the ground. She wiped her nose on her shabby, gray jacket. But she could not face the bird's eyes.

"Does it bother you that I fly?" The bird asked.

That remark nearly broke her to pieces. A tear came to her eyes as she rubbed them off on her sleeve, and then she looked directly at her shoes. Then she opened up to the bird. "I wish I could fly. I'd go straight up and never come back. I'm too old to fly anyway," she cried.

Sarah concentrated on her shoe and listened to the bird's suggestions on what to do. She would usually use its ideas on what to do in each event of her life.

"Why don't you kill one of them?" The bird oddly suggested. This was strange because the bird had never told her to do this before. "Come on. You can't tell me you never thought of killing someone."

I never killed anyone. The thought felt like a stab in the back. Sarah never liked thinking of violence. But once she contemplated it felt a little good. *I do!* She admitted. *I do want to kill everyone in there.* She remembered the funny faces all around her before she would wait to go to sleep in the institute at night.

"Then just do it," the bird suggested. He spread his wings horizontally. He then closed them. Then he nodded at Sarah. He waited patiently for an answer. "Just kill them. Who cares?" Said the bird.

Sarah contemplated for a while. She leaned down on her legs and moved back and forth. "I've made my decision. I'll do it!" She decided.

It wasn't more than minutes before she was in her Psyche unit, and she sat at her usual table. The same drawn out and pressured feelings surfaced. But there was no way to let it go. Then she remembered what the blackbird said. The thought was chilling at first. It was stuck in her head, and she couldn't get rid of it.

Something caught Sarah's attention like no other thing in her past. *What is...that?* It was dull and dirty with clay, but it still glistened in her mind. She reached out and cupped it with her left hand. Then she grabbed it, and when she did an enormous chill went right up her arm. Then her eyes glared all around the room. She was a monster running around with a knife! Then she stabbed and pulled for a moment on something, and she had no idea who it was. But it was human flesh. The punishment would have been prison.

Sarah was strapped to a wheelchair at the center of a large room. The patients tried not to catch her eye. She could see them looking at times. Suddenly light matter dripped to Sarah's chin. More came up much thicker, and spilled to her chest. Then something light and timid came into her mind. It was the blackbird. It was flying through the sky, and it was alone. It was a light and timid touch. And it was dismal as if the bird was lost.

"Are they dead?" the bird asked with enlightenment. The light touch of the bird brought a tear to Sarah's eye. "Someone is dead. But I don't know who it was," she answers. Then with no control she let a hard cry. "I'll never leave here now. I'll never be on the outside. I'll never see you again."

Memories, as common, come into Sarah's mind. The cold Winters with the Blackbird. The smoke from the chimneys on the houses across the street, she recalls. She sees a warm coat and a cup of coffee, watching the snow on the trees. She remembers the fall leaves and all the changes of the season, the bathing sun and the fresh flowers. Yet she realizes that these things would be gone soon.

The only thing she would dream for would be the return of the blackbird.

She wants someone she could talk to and confide in. She wants someone to share food with and watch.

"Blackbird?" Sarah searches for the bird. "Come and find me?"

Sarah leans overlooks outside the window. She sees a tiny thing at a distance as she squints her eyes. She moves the wheelchair closer. *He will return*!

Suddenly the bird appeared. Swooping towards the window, only to disappear. Then he came back into Margaret's mind.

"Are you committed?" asked the bird. The bird didn't seem surprised.

"Yes I am," concluded Sarah.

Suddenly, as Sarah turns her head, she found the blackbird sitting outside the window. Every night, before

Sarah went to bed, she and the blackbird would talk about anything that happened that day. Sometimes it was over breakfast, and others with a warm cup of coffee, or at night before Sarah went to sleep.

Chapter Seven

The Couch

The red, rusty rugs and heavy furniture rotted with moldy colors was the first scene in office. The man in the chair was thin from nose to stomach. He sat with legs spread apart, leaning forward, and looking straight into the eyes of Albert. Albert was a prisoner of the Artific Institution, a place for insane. Then the man sat back in his chair, tapped his pen to his lip, and smiled. His nose seemed to catch the orders of the rotten wood. Albert sat sternly, yet sloped from the waist up.

The man gestured by opening his hands, and closing. "This must be the most exciting moment of your Life!" He nodded his head in courteously, yet still seemed to be rather imposing.

The next scene was almost a horror picture. And in the man's eye, it seemed to be exhilarating, being a beginner. Albert's subjectivity was becoming very objective. His hands were stiff with fingers spread apart, resting on his legs. His legs were held close together and at times one would twitch. His face was completely expressionless, except for that of years locked away in an institution. He was blunt and "Am I making you nervous Albert?" the doctor, the man in the room, inquired. "You seem nervous, as if you were being instigated." The smile returned to the doctor's face.

But the answer was rather blunt in itself. "No," was all that was answered.

Of course Albert and the doctor were trying to communicate. But it seemed as though all Albert was doing was watching, as if he was contemplating something much more important, and interesting. So there he sat, merely watching motions then listening to words.

The doctor eventually noticed. His inexperience became quite obvious as he finally noticed an expression on Albert's face of exhaustion. Not knowing quite what to do, he allowed Albert to lye on the couch. But Albert simply would not move from his chair.

The doctor's next comment seemed very intimidating. It caused a slight exacerbation, which became noticed in Albert's eyes. "Do you not want to be here?"

the doctor began. "Would you like to return to your room?"

Again, Albert's response was blunt. "No" is all that was said.

For a moment there was silence. But this was swell because it gave time for the doctor to study the patient objectively. It seemed as though he was deaf. He wasn't studying, concentrating or listening. He was merely looking down at his feet.

He didn't even seem like he was contemplating. As he looked into the doctor's eye, the same was noticed, yet their eyes did meet. It was as though he was allowing the doctor to study him. Then, it was at this point that the doctor realized this patient was severely demented.

"Why don't you speak? Cat got your tongue? The doctor makes a mistake again. Albert's eyes rolled and closed. Then his head dropped. He looks at the doctor from one eye.

"Ma, My ...No," was all that was answered. Then came a sentence. "The doctor said...No.

Feebly, the doctor searches for words. "What doctor, tell me more."

Also feebly, Albert blurts an answer, "The doctor."

"The doctor said that a cat has not caught your tongue," the doctor replied humorously.

Albert opens and closes his hand. "Yes," he replies with a humorous smile caught on his face. Then he merely shakes his head. Quite suddenly, Albert seems to look about the room as if startled. He turns and looks at the door behind him.

"What's wrong Albert," the doctor inquires quite contently. What's behind the door?" He points to the only door in the room.

"The room," Albert replies, sort of leaving the doctor wondering.

"What room, Albert? Which room, the doctor's?" The doctor must wait a moment for Albert to answer.

"My room," Albert blurted out, again leaving the doctor wondering.

"That's what the doctor said," Albert completed.

Suddenly, almost unpersuasively, the doctor began to jot down notes.

He looked to Albert for his expression. He searched for his excitement. Albert was very blunt. He peered at the pen with an unfamiliar expression. His attention stayed for one moment. He began to look around the room nervously.

"Albert, I need to tell you that I want to help." The doctor introduced.

Albert looked upwards in contemplation.

"What do you want Albert?" the doctor asked.

Albert thought for one moment and answered, "My room."

Albert was escorted back to his doctor's district. He glanced at faces that seemed to rectify the sins of the world. Then he paused his traveling to see the doctor, sitting at his desk, with a bible in his hands. Albert returned to his room to his favorite place. It was his chair by the window where he would stare at the fields for hours. He lustfully dreamt of the couch.

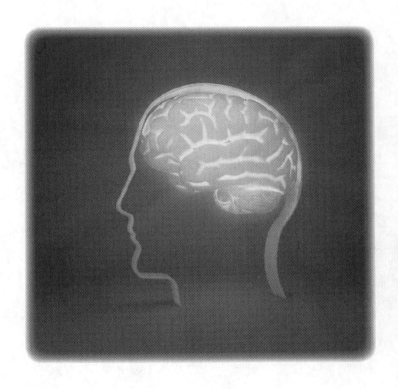

Chapter Eight

At Night

At night I hear a mouse,
Augustus fills the light,
and as the mouse is dead,
my heart pounds with
    delight.

At night I hear a bird,
who sings a sky of blue,
it's bluest in the night,
my mind feels
    something new.

At night the Winter is cold,
while floating down a
    stream,
the coldness heals my back,
and this I tend to dream.

At night the evening is
    warm,
as I swim in my pond,
the water may not be fresh,
but within myself I bond.

At night I am in black water,
around me is lost land,
I dig a hole in the ground,
for the water soothes my
    hand.

And in this night of
    dreaming,
I build the largest house,
and in the house I'm soothed,
and settled, because I killed
the mouse

Finding Myself

I sit in metal furniture,
My arms are locked in
    chains,
My mind is unresponsive,
Except for in my pain.

Life around me growing,
In beauty I can't see,
As I sit in motionless,
Around me all is free.

I feel the whip upon my
    back,
It beats me on and on,
If any light shines on me,
Quickly it is gone.

I can't see the colors,
Or the sight of
    something new,

I cannot do anything,
For there is nothing I
    can do.

Sometimes my arm
    enlightens,
And spins around my side,
But soon it goes away,
For I feel that I must hide.

As my mind feels open,
To see what I can do,
My eyes begin to focus,
Incredibly a cue.

Then I feel the passion,
As I sit and tell, my word
And one day when it
    happens,
I'll fly free like a bird.

I Place My Feet

I place my feet together,
on journey to forever.
I'm forced to climb some stairs,
As if someone not cares,
And make a sound like feathers.
I look to see alignment,
Remembering confinement.
I look to my first step,
remembering my rep,
and see the darkened diamond.
I begin to climb stairs,
And say all my bewares,
But they are much too steep,
My eyes almost do weep,
Because nobody cares.
I can hardly stand,
The railing on my hand,
My feet to heavy,
But my weapon ready,
To enter in their land.
With hand to meet,
I place my feet,
I move it hard,
The winning card,
And go to get a treat.

Inside The Mind

I do hate the summer,
The sun shines too bright,
I'd rather freeze completely,
And feel the coldest bite.

Isolation is the choice,
I follow in this world,
To see what I can do in life,
Is like glancing on a pearl.

You are warm and dry,
I am cold and wet,
I am said to suffer,
Though I have not suffered yet.

The coldness breaks my body,
All except my heart,
What may come to be,
When it's time for me to part?

Oh the cold is good at night,
You cannot see where you are,
You cannot see who is after you,
In the sun you see so far.

Now I'm going deep inside,
Where you will never find,
Why am I to stay here,
So I'll reach deep inside my mind.

Not Somewhere In The Air

Beyond the Earth we live,
Yes there I'd like to be,
Far from everybody else,
To see no land or sea.

Geography is a bore you
    know,
The Earth to dry for me,
In total endless darkness,
Pitch black but yet so free.

My feet not stand on
    anything,
For when I see the fire,
It's the most I ever felt,
And as I see inside my self,
My soul begins to melt.

I never knew a better way,
Than making this my world,
To see inside the fore more,
To see my future life.

Enlightened I stare some
    time,
And it begins to warm,
But never is it better than,
To feel my evil storm.

Assure you, it's not my
    master,
For the fire is so small,
But as I stare inside,
I feel somebody's call.

May it be the fire,
Or may it be my mind,
The feeling is deep inside
    myself,
This must be what I find

And as I look around
    myself,
My dreams come while I
    stare.

Around me are the stars,
So timid too they light,
They help me free in
    dreaming,
My body loses fright.

Where is this empty place?
I will not say beware,
It's living deep inside my
    mind,
Not somewhere in the air.

Deep Inside The Fire

I see more in a fire,
Then just a way of light,
I do not understand you,
A fire is not to fight.

A fire is intriguing,
For when I look inside,
It shows me my own spirit,
I tell it I have lied.

For when I see the fire,
It's the most I ever felt,
And as I see inside my self,
My soul begins to melt.

I never knew a better way,
Than making this my
    world,
To see inside the fore more,

To see my future life.

Enlightened I stare some
    time,
And it begins to warm,
But never is it better than,
To feel my evil storm.

Assure you, it's not my
    master,
For the fire is so small,
But as I stare inside,
I feel somebody's call.

May it be the fire,
Or may it be my mind,
The feeling is deep inside
    myself,
This must be what I find.

Sea Dove

A line between divides,
Beautiful misty air,
Below the ocean blueness,
The sky above they share.

The beach meets there
    also,
With no tall hill to climb,
Softness on my bare feet,
And then the scene they
    find.

Closer the water reaches,
But by me it will pass,
As I walk in this painting,
The sea and shore at last.

My body cools in
    windiness,
Around me I am Free,

I divide into the ocean,
And feel the heavy sea.

I swoop up out of the
    water,
I'm flying like a dove,
In and out I wonder,
The sea and I make love.

Now I reach the sand,
And look back on this
    place,
Everywhere is beautiful,
Any way I face.

I/m very much alone,
Except the seagulls dare,
And now I leave my ocean,
As if it didn't care.

Sunset Night

The sun begins to set,
Through the clouds it breaks,
What a bleakest day,
The sun brings us to wake.

The stillness is so light,
All around becomes the
    same,
The fields and on the ground,
Yes everything around.

The sky is gray and gloomy,
Except for this scene,
It stops my mind from
Wondering
With the trickle of a dream.

It makes me look around
    myself,
It becomes a relaxing thing,
It is almost, almost
    wakes me,
Though soon night it will
    bring.

It's almost like a picture,
With something noticed
    more,
Or maybe to the heavens,
It becomes a door.

Maybe someone is
    watching,
From the sky above,
Maybe it's a painting for,
Two people making love.

Now as I look at things,
My eyes don not dart
    around,
This lovely presentation,
Is darting out the sound.

So that now my thought,
Is very smooth and light,
It is still and open,
Just that sunset night.

The Chimes

By Susan M Cane

Embalmed,
evaluated.
That's the same.
Implicitly, and
conditionally.
Always seems to be.

Food smells worn on
   demented people,
insinuated.
Drastically, sinfully
   insinuated
that it is they,
and this is not the truth,
It is sinful!

Then the sights the looks.
Then the nights the days in
   seclusion,
Then the small rooms and
   beds.
Then the evil the sinful
   looks,
and sights
and lives.

The sights!
They are speaking,
They are listening,
Seeing, watching, speaking
Stop it.
Go away the devil!
Faces speak!

The looks!
The jeers and faces smear.
The haunt and taunt taunt,
The thought of release
Outside,
the natures.
I'd abide the natures!

The papers with no words!
The treatment of absurd.
Rainy nights.
Gorgy appetites
Bed times.
Death chimes.

The Knife

Do you at times wonder,
Where began our pain?
Why if we were born to God
Do we put ourselves to
    shame?

Why is it that when we are
Confident
Our world is colored bright?
And when we lose this credit,
Our bodies dye in fright?

Is it as though maybe,
That this credit we enjoy,
Is life itself in a form,
So we desert the Lord?

Is this the way the lucky,
Grow in higher form?
Is this why the strongest,
Are always this way born?

Is it true to suffer,
Is to be a lower way?
Though Jesus chose to do
    this,
Until the rising day?

Now if your performance,
For the higher race,
Fits their liking,
And then begins a chase.

The chase is our own
    suffering,
Fighting as the poor,
But never do we seem to,
Open deep within a core.

Without its understanding,
To live their way of life,
It becomes to happen,
And then we use the knife.

The Then Return

It is purposeful,
a domain,
to fame,
to trust,
to honor.
But then a return!

Then return,
The smell of musk,
The fresh smell of clothes,
The golden ring,
The patients who sing,
with no return,
can't return.

But they can!
Because the then return,
Would destroy sympathy,
The need,
The urge,
and then comes victory.

To do the Then Return,
You need things.
Fate, patience, no pride,
pride is selfish.
A walk,
in the park,
contemplating what's next.

What's next?
To do the Then Return!
We could return…
No jealousy.

The Then Return!
The Then Return!
Swing an learn,
clap and turn,
Sing and churn,
What's going on?

The Then Return!
Rise and see,
what I you can be!
The Then Return,
inside of me,
so all can see,
me Then Return.

The fiscal age,
Of love in rage,
Of new blank page,
The Then Return!
The Then Return!
Dance and churn!

Manic Depression.
Session.
Impressions lesson.
Beckon.
No words from mouth.
Smaller, smaller.
Over.

No shame!
Or potential,
that we can learn!

Together In A Fantasy

The bird is clothed with
   feathers,
The blackest jacket on,
The orange suited dress
   shirt,
And wings are ever long.

The fence surrounds this
   fielding,
And together they are fit,
Fascinating seeing it,
Watching as I sit.

It reminds me of England,
Where birds are often
   born,
In the land of prejudice,
A land ruled by a lord.

It reminds me of a mystery,
Of poems often born,
Like a bird named Raven,
Who seats in drier corn.

The bird can be of freedom,
Of flying in the air,
It can wake you in the morn,
Yet sit in trees of bare.

It can remind you of many
   things,
Like land of hardly all,
Flying over nothingness,
Yet always give a call.

Together in my fantasy,
Of freedom and alone,
To fly and see no civilized,
Where only few will roam.

The magic of the feathered
   coat,
The mystery of the flight,
The freedom of the
   daytime,
And the dismal of the
   night.

Without Something

Isn't it unpleasant,
Sometimes such a shame,
To survive a world,
By playing such a game.

Yes day by day we suffer,
And told this is the way,
Of which we must exist,
Every single day.

I am feeling such a gloom,
What I wanted would not stay
How was I to ever know,
That would read what I say.

I almost lost a more real thing,
Something you cannot lose,
One who guides your way of life,
That is as you're born to chose.

When I found it wasn't gone,
To Jesus I did speak,
Thanking him for not losing,
Whom without I'd be so weak.

I smile as I think of this,
How still it's by my side,
I promise that with this thing,
I would never die.

Without Something

Isn't it unpleasant,
Sometimes such a shame,
To survive a world,
By playing such a game.

Yes day by day we suffer,
And told this is the way,
Of which we must exist,
Every single day.

I am feeling such a gloom,
What I wanted would not stay
How was I to ever know,
That would read what I say.

I almost lost a more real thing,
Something you cannot lose,
One who guides your way of life,
That is as you're born to chose.

When I found it wasn't gone,
To Jesus I did speak,
Thanking him for not losing,
Whom without I'd be so weak.

I smile as I think of this,
How still it's by my side,
I promise that with this thing,
I would never die.

Holly, Holly Sunday

Susan M Cane
OCT 24 2010

My feet hit the pavement,
to rid the world of Trident,
and make less all confinement,
Never swear,
never dare.

My Holly, Holly Sunday,
close your hands and pray,
Jesus comes one day.
He will be here,
and hold all dear.

Its on the Holy Sunday,
the word to forgive will say,
all will not stay.
Here it comes,
to all sons.

Sunday is Holy Repent,
all the words are sent,
all who pay the rent.
The Gentiles seek,
To be redeemed.

And on that Holy Sunday,
when Peace keeps the trees,
and all the aesthetic scenes.
Of the world,
of God.

Imagining Concrete

Walking up a wall today,
It moves from east to west,
Now it moves so I must
  crawl,
It's bringing me no peace.

Now it's moving very far,
I hardly hold grip,
If I hold on any longer,
My back and legs will rip.

The rock is cold and wet,
It's not easy holding on,
If I close my eyes to tight,
The decision will be gone.

If I stopped I could relax,
And find that I could sleep,
But my will is to stay on,
The fighting I must keep.

See moving back and forth,
Is nothing to concrete,
I'm imaging this,

It's something incomplete.

Everyday I do this thing,
And do this so do you,
Decision is not an
  easy way,
It's something we must do.

Confusion is a way in life,
As I can't keep up too long,
Is east the way to go,
Or am I choosing wrong.

Yes, back and forth I move,
So that I can hardly think,
It's moving quicker now,

Labor and Work

The Irish to Irish,
the pub, drink and fetch.
The Italian Italians,
that fight like a retch.
They labor and work,
American.

Down in the work house,
almost a prison,
thrown away visions.
Down the asylum,
push to get by them,
give them provisions.

The Patriots are flying,
soon for War be dying,
all nations defying.
Hitler has scored,
England just snored,
apocalypse ignored.

But eyes they still gleam,
how happy they seem,
an American dream.
We all work hard,
even when scarred,
Labor and work barred,
American

Now I Know I Will

I feel the cold of Death,
there is no looking in his eyes,
there is no movement of his
body,
no never will he rise.

He does not hear a sound.
He does not breath a breath.
But although he seems this way.
He feels a better death.

His skin of blue I notice,
Yet his eyes content,
Yes I am sure of something,
To where his death was sent.

His eyes are also pleasant,
With Jesus he must be,
Although I see the coldness,
He must be so free.

I wonder of his purity,
Or if he ever sinned.
Did he choose my way of life,
Of moving through the wind?

For this wind is in his coldness,
As if he lived the chill,
And now I am glad I know
This,
For now I know I will.

Strauss Was My Father

Susan Marie Cane
June 26 2011

Like when I dissected a
    frog'ger,
and Science became
    farther,
and man became smarter.
Time was being harder,
and inside my mind,
Strauss was my Father.

It began with illusions,
and mental, mind ridding
    confusions,
and bulging contusions.
Life was delusions,
and in this entity
nothing was surprising,
just amusing.

I knew it had to be him,
my nose and face smell
    like gin,

my hair sweaty with sin.
My laughter at the bin
of noises,
My Father above in trim.

So I played and played, and
    played,
all throughout the day,
who cares what they say,
even coins that they pay,
cannot rise above,
My fathers day

Like the interval of rising,
and your enemies
    declining,
I did a little finding.
As in the past,
and all used last,
I used my father,
Strauss Was My Father.

Susan! Susan! Susan!

What was that?
Oh, nothing.
There it goes again!
It's someone,
else,
Just working.
I am just about to sleeping,
When this dame sound
    keeps a creeping.
Susan, will you please
    listen?
We believe in your
    mission,
And all we need is
    commission.
Let us do to your
    submission.
We'll take any condition.
Susan! Susan!
Please listen.

You can tell us again your
    vision,
It's not just superstition,
Your horrible disposition.
You see, Susan!
I can hardly breath,
My heart it pumps in need,
Its like I have not feed,
Myself,
Indeed.
I look around the room,
To find the face of gloom,
And very pretty soon,
I laugh like a balloon.
This person came to soon.
Susan, Susan, Susan!
I completely ignore,
And plan out for the store,
I'm certain locked the door,
To be unruly sure,
I hear their call no more.

In The Darkest Moments...

Sleeping in a room,
With seven faces gloom.
Eyes bounce around,
Connected and abound.
I had a good night sleep,
Only to wake to the creep.
Rested people seek,
A happy little peek.
While watching a TV,
to see the others be,
I eat a piece of cheese.
I learn of wallabies.
But should be learning all the keys,
all the dreams,
all the seas,
all the scenes,
and all the meanings.
Then the Kings and Queens,
Laughing at a moment scream,
although they will redeem.
But in a sense of religion,
And the man with the pigeon.
Your happy face falls,
When you see the clause,
of heads hitting walls.
So I reach extend my claws,
In the darkest moments.

Waiting For The Call

Up upon this mountain,
Oh, I dream of it so well,
It isn't really heaven,
It's a little close to hell.

Around bright lights flashing,
It's closest to no sun.
Now I'd like to dwell on it,
Oh, this is so much fun.

There's a space between us,
Myself and this queer thing,
It enlightens me so much,
But, I want the call to sing.

By back is hard and aching,
Waiting for the call,
And now my back releases,
And now I'll walk along.

I walk through a garden,
All plain in black or white,
The thing watches me,
Again I dream of night.

Climbing up the mountain,
You think it is a house,
It's walking in the world alone,
Trying not to kill a mouse.

The Empty Table
By Susan M Cane

In an early, summer morn,
Fixing leg pants torn,
Feeding first born,
Wooden table
not set.

Grab the silver wear,
Mother sewing shirt tare,
Reminded not to swear,
Still smiles,
not gone yet.

Sit up right, and sight
will be on mother's right,
And at night,
Put away the jet,
And sleep.

Then grow faster then
    seemed,
All mother's teachings
    redeemed,
All her future's dreams,
Just to go and get,
And leave.

This seems,
To be her dreams,

Wasted,
Hasted,
Thrown away.

She drinks,
It stinks the hall ways,
It incarcerates her,
Never bears,
Never wears.

Children smoke,
Pot, but not, not
Not enough,
Not enough,
To go on.

Be strong, strong
For such a long time,
Kind, can't find it,
Grasp it,
Cast it.

The table set again,
When, just remembering,
Now and then, crying
Trying, trying,
Dying.

I am lying,
No one knows,
I am dying,
No one comes,
Shows,
acknowledges.

The table legs.
Hobble.
As she sits.
Its possible,
she's deep and heavy,
devastated.

Alone she eats,
separated feet,
hands grasp,

the ham and meat,
indulging,
alone.

Tears reflect memories,
Hard cry.
Treasuries.
Never mean
anything
anymore.

Cleaning up dishes,
wishes examining mind.
This is why
she survives
lonely,
He is dead.

The Past in the Millennium

By Susan M Cane

Mistaken for a horseless carriage,
New rules made for marriage,
The Nazis leave the barrage,
No one left to honor.

From candles to data COM,
Rules break Uncle Tom,
Signification the Atom bomb,
Right is taken from ponder.

Eisenhower is blocked away,
He's been forfeited just today,
He promised we would be okay,
Be now we only wonder.

Kennedy was a deepest hope,
His grip left the rope,
But now his name is how to cope,
With no one any fonder.

Now we're faced with nuclear choke,
To never be the reign of Stoke,
The chain of armies broke,
In The Past of the Millennium.

Then All My Dreams Came True

By Susan M Cane

It was a wonder.
Ponder, I ponder
The wonder
Of it all.

Forever, ever,
Never leave,
Whether, or not,
you need.

Never make it anyway,
They say,
The day,
I was sent in.

Ill forever,
Together, you cannot
Sever, sever,
Sever will not preclude,
The illness,
They said.

We doubt, we doubt,
You shout, you bought,
They through out,
The papers.

Lifeless years, tears,
Mirrors,
Fears,
Neglected and projecting,
Peers, no sights,
No visions.

No rights,
The mighty, fights
of life.
And I've
Injected twice!

Then asked what I could
    do, they laugh.
That's when all my dreams
    came true.

The truth, it's the truth,
see it
Spills in from youth,
The feeling,
Of dealing,
Erupted.

My smiles,
But the others miles,
Away, my death,
But my breath,
They wonder.

From God above,
The love,
Streamed in,
A dream,
Came to mind and stayed.

My potential, the central,
Part of my mind,
Kind, find.
Find the crime,
In it all.

It's the crime,
That sometimes,
Does not sublime,
To the kind'
Of people you are.

Live in the spirit
And never move,
the dear feelings,
of subjectivity.

If you never,
Receive the endeavor,
in this horror, world
of spit, fat, or any other,
borrow the world of God.

For God
Is the endeavor,
the world of words
that make sense
repent and receive
God.

And in the Darkness,
and the strangeness, eats
the devil,
Himself.
He tortures the soul.

The jurisdiction, judge,
He is,
always will be.
But to God,
justice,
Is love.

To find,
The sign,
Against the side,
Their crime,
Involves.

The swine,
In time,
Will never find,
Even though,
There's room for love.

And as I gaze,
At the maze,
the haze,
I find room for love.

Never, can
I ever,
Let go,
Of anything that stays.

They were appalled, they saw it.
That's when all my dreams came true.

It doesn't matter,
where you live,
who you are,
where you go,
Devil gives
You nothing in return.

And to learn,
the turn,
of time,
Gives glide,
To the mind.

Chapter Nine

Excerpt From Jake's Revenge

by Susan M Cane

Jake was manic-depressive. From what family he had that was alive, nobody came to visit. Did he mind? He did mind and it made him very upset. He never really made a friend except for greeting other patients at the supper table. Friends would only make him depressed, so he stayed away.

Alle entered the day hall followed by Nurse Rendy. "Stop, stop, stop, stop," he would mutter as nurse Rendy tried to catch him and get the medicine shot over with. Alle seemed to always be getting shots. It was like he got one for everything he did, not just once a week like Jake. He got all kinds too.

Jake was usually very rebellious. He would often be very sarcastic with the nurses. She finally caught him with the help of other staff members. They strapped him down and gave him the shot anyway. Then they just left him there. He lied still though and would never make a noise. Then the nurses would just sit and talk or laugh at times.

Especially nurse Rendy. She was the one who made all the voices.

Nobody really seemed to care about what was going in this hospital. It was as though they couldn't. It was some kind of impairment that closed their minds. You didn't look around. You would look straight ahead or down. It was so racy in there that your mind quickens to the point that you can't think straight. Then you get confused which really used to be frustrating to Jake. But if he waited it would just pass by.

Later the staff would sit around the table and talk. People hung from their chairs, disgusted and exhausted. Eyes were gazing and minds were only wondering. Some were in wheelchairs; others were not. But all together, they suffered. There was nothing but stillness. There was medication. But because of it, there was allot of vomiting also. Weakness grew and all was dismal. There were arms up around heads and shoulders. Sometimes there would be a cry.

Anyhow, one day came Doctor Abraham. He had come to see Jake. As he went to sit, Jake would not face him. After trying to get a response, Abraham continued to tell him his exciting news. Jake looked at the Doctor as Abraham went through Jake's chart. "You know pal with allot of paperwork, I could get you out of here," Doctor said. Jake didn't trust him. Doctors had always hurt him in the past. "Sign this and I'll have an attorney come tomorrow morning."

Three days later, Jake was released to an outpatient organization. He lived in a section eight that meant the state would pay for an apartment for him. It was a small apartment. But it was better than nurse Rendy. It was quiet but somehow it was incomplete. Something felt like a scar in his head and it was so irritating.

He stared vaguely at the ceiling. Smoking a cigarette, he was finally relaxed. He thought of nurse Rendy. All he could remember was her walking up and down the hall with such an echoing laughter. It used to make him feel inferior. He wanted to make her stop but she wouldn't. It haunted him and he felt nothing but fear. His mind would constantly pressure him to an anger he could not control.

His mind lessened before their loud noises. He gave in to a state that was so synchronized that all other emotion wasn't there. Evil took over sanity and he just gazed in the small closed in walls. His mind was aching and he wanted it soothed! He just couldn't think of how. His anger raged.

At this point his eyes glared around the room thinking of the long time he spent in the hospital. He would do this alone, not to tell anyone. They'd tease him again if they knew. His rape, his emotional rape was still the plaster in their creation. It agitated him until he was forced to relieve it by thinking of revenge. A revenge he had never felt or thought of before.

He pictured her face. He imagined her. She was haunting him again. The Hallucination kept repeating," You'll never leave here! You're here for ever now." The laughter was louder and louder. Jake moved his head back and forth until finally, the Hallucination disappeared. His eyes were still and tortured.

He lay back out of breath. He saw her over and over. "Is this insane?" He yelled to himself. He calmed in the thought of an ending. He folds his hands on his stomach and drifted off unto insanity. This time his eyes waved around the room, but it was very unfamiliar. But it did feel good and he wished for it to stay a while.

The next day, he wakes from a nightmare. She was there in his dream. She was everywhere and there was no way to make her go! He tried drinking some whiskey he had bought in the town area. He took a few sips and lye back. Sweat was on his forehead as he felt the alcohol run in his vein. The bottle slipped from his hands. His arm began to shake. He was haunted and felt that he couldn't escape. What was left to do?

He took some medication that Doctor Abraham had prescribed. That was better again. He drifted off unto a tranquil, content state. His mind saw Abraham and he closed his eyes. The drug circulated and then there was a positive notion. His mind cleared, but only for now. The medicine never hid the voices for long.

The pill felt so good. But he needed more. He didn't want to heal it. He wanted to soothe it. "Pleasure," he thought. But what kind of pleasure was there? What kind of pleasure? What could he do to soothe it? Soothing would feel so good but whenever he thought this way he would panic. He was so confused. He wished he didn't have a mind.

Next evening Jake is watching television. It wasn't color, but it was a nice set. A woman caught his attention. She was taking off her clothes for another man. Instantly, he thought of nurse Rendy. He began to fantasize.

He liked thinking of Nurse Rendy. This was soothing. This was pleasure. "To rape her," he thought. No, that was not the answer. "To kill her!" Yes! That was it! He paused. His mind knew this would do it. He spends some time thinking and planning.

He knew when she would be leaving the hospital. "I'd better hurry or it will be late" There was a knife in the kitchen that would be perfect for killing nurse Rendy. He removed the knife from the drawer. The knife shined as he looked at it. It was long and perfectly sharp. It will feel so good.

The night was dark and gloomy. It was almost as though somebody knew what he was doing. That didn't bother him. He'd kill nurse Rendy anyway. As he approached the hospital, the knife was in his jacket, held close to his side. Just the closeness of the knife felt good. It would feel even better to use it.

He hid along the side of a door where she we would be leaving. There was a perfect place to jump out and kill nurse Rendy. So he waited patiently with the knife in both hands. His face stiffened with determination. His coat was as black as the night. The air was as cold as the knife in his hands.

Sure enough, Nurse Rendy walked through the door. Violently he leaped from the bushes and began to stab her with the knife. Each stabbing felt so good that his arm moved mechanically. The blood soothed his mind. As she screamed his body became limp and slowly he continued to stab. Slowly almost deliberately, she fell to the ground. As Jake looked curiously, he saw a slight dripping of blood in her mouth. But the sensations left in his arms would not allow him to quit.

As she lye on the cold pavement outside the corridor, he sat before the bleeding body with one leg stretched out. With wrists on the back of the knife and hands stiff, he continued to stab. His young face and wimpy hands were stern with confidence. And there, lying before him was a dead nurse Rendy.

People rushed down the corridor and outside to catch Jake. He didn't wrestle or put up a fight. A nurse took the knife from his hand that was dripping wet with nurse Rendy's blood. His body was so soothed that he had thought the Devil was inside his soul. Again he smiled. There was no reason to fret. He didn't have to; nurse Rendy was dead!

Two very strong nurses grabbed each of his arms. This is when Jake began to fight. But since his body was much to small and young, he could only slightly struggle. His sneakers skid on the floor as his legs were straight out, one after the other he kicked. As they carried him throughout the hospital halls, in order to lock him in a room and await the police, he began to scream wildly. He seemed, by the others, like a wild animal in a complete rage. As they put him in an isolated room, be continued to bang on the window in an out rage. In time, he sat in a corner.

His legs were held closely against his chest. He stares at his red, torn sneakers. He begins to quickly shuffle his feet. Suddenly Eddie, a close friend, appeared at the window. Jake looked into his eye, jeered his teeth and smiled.

Eddie moved his fingers at his eyes. Jake jeers again. But suddenly a staff member pushes Eddie away and checks Jake, and leaves.

The hearing was held for a few weeks. But since Jake was young and severely mentally ill, he was only committed to a child's institution. He was also allowed visits. Therefore Eddie would frequently come to see him. They would swap baseball cards, play chess and mostly talk about rock groups and football. Eddie would usually stay for the full visit.

Jake stared for a moment at Eddie's eyes as they sit on the floor and swap cards. Eddie notices. "What's wrong?" Eddie inquires.

"What's wrong with your eyes?" Jake answers Eddies question. He seriously and angrily looks into Eddie's eyes.

Eddie looks astonished. "What's wrong with you, man?" Eddie knew Jake very well. He puts his cards in his shirt pocket. "What do you mean, what's wrong with my eyes?" Jake begins to laugh hysterically. He starts to throw cards at Eddie's head.

"Hell! I am out of here!" Eddies gets up and walks to the door. He grabs his coat and walks into the hall. Jake chases him, jumps on him and begins to hit his face severely.

"Hell with you! Hell with you!" Jake repeats as his fists begin to mark Eddie's face. Pulling Eddie's hair, be yells again, "Wimp! Bastard!"

Staff members pulled him off. As Jake was finally released from this situation, Eddie could hardly get up. When his face was shown, all could see he was again astonished with Jake.

"You're crazy man! You're nuts!" Eddies catches his breath.

"That's right man! I am a Looney! I am crazy! Woo-woo! Woo-woo!

Jake teases Eddie as he is escorted from the unit. He suddenly says," Hey man!

You coming over tomorrow?" As Eddie looks back, Jake jeers his teeth.

Eddies shakes his head and leaves, yet returned the next day to visit.

As Jake had expected, Eddie returned the next day to visit. Jake was just finishing his breakfast. As Eddie expected, Jake began to tease. He set a buttered roll in front of Eddie's face.

"Eat it!" Jake joked as he became hysterical. He points his finger and could not stop laughing. Eddie merely stared humorously. Then his eyes dropped.

He made a sorrowful look at Jake. Then he made his decision. I got up from the table, and left the room. The next day Jake waited for Eddie, but he never returned.

Jake sat in the corner of the room, feet up on a chair before him. He was itching hid thumb with his fore finger. On his face his eyes had a pleasant smile. He seemed very contemplating, laughing. He lit a cigarette and watched the room and television, with eyes glaring contently on every motion in the room.